Written by
Katherine Pebley O'Neal

Illustrated by
Laura Huliska-Beith

Grandpa Grumpy's Family

ZONDERkidz

ZONDERVAN.com/
AUTHORTRACKER
follow your favorite authors

The Lord looks deep down inside every heart.
– I Chronicles 28:9

Grandpa Grumpy's Family
Copyright © 2008 by Katherine Pebley O'Neal
Illustrations © 2008 by Laura Huliska-Beith

Requests for information should be addressed to:
Zonderkidz, Grand Rapids, Michigan 49530

Library of Congress Cataloging-in-Publication Data: Applied for

ISBN-10: 0-310-70956-5
ISBN-13: 978-0-310-70986-2

Art direction & Design: Merit Alderink
Editor: Amy DeVries

Printed in China

08 09 10 11 • 6 5 4 3 2 1

To Kelly,
who is only grumpy
some of the time

-K.P.O.

For Mom and Dad:
Thank you for all the
love and patience
you gave your loud and
messy children!

-L.H.B.

"Breakfast!" called Gregory's mom. Gregory ran downstairs. He could smell bacon—his favorite thing for breakfast.

"My bacon is burned," grumped Grandpa Grumpy.

"You take it, Gregory." Grandpa put two perfectly cooked pieces of bacon on Gregory's plate.

"Thanks!" said Gregory.

Grandpa was grumpy, but Gregory loved him anyway.

Grumble Grumble Grumble

Gregory was excited because Grandpa was
taking him to the zoo today with his friends from
church. After breakfast, they were ready to go.

Grandpa Grumpy picked up his umbrella and filled his pocket with butterscotch candies.

"We'll probably be late," he said with a frown. "Let's get going."
"Okay," said Gregory. "Bye, Mom!"
"Have fun!" said Gregory's mom, and she kissed them both good-bye.
"We'll try, but it looks like rain," Grandpa grouched.

They met Gregory's friends Annie, Dusty, and Rory at the zoo entrance. Grandpa handed out butterscotch candies to each one.

"They're too sweet for me," complained Grandpa. "You kids take them."

"Thank you," the children said.

First, they visited the baboons. They were Annie's favorite, but she was way in the back of the group.

"Baboons are too smelly for me," grumped Grandpa Grumpy. "Annie, you take my spot up in front."

"Gee, thanks, Mr. Grumpy!" said Annie.

Next, they rode the camels. They were Rory's favorite,
but the rides were very short.

"Camels are too bumpy for me," complained Grandpa.
"Why don't you take my turn, Rory?"
"Gee, thanks, Mr. Grumpy!" yelled Rory.

When the kids got hungry, they stopped for ice cream. Dusty really wanted a chocolate ice cream cone but he had forgotten to bring his money.

"Ice cream is too messy for me," grumbled Grandpa. "You can have my cone, Dusty."

"Yum! Thanks, Mr. Grumpy," Dusty said eagerly.

They walked from one end of the zoo to the other and saw every animal there. They even had their faces painted after lunch.

Signpost: ELEPHANT, BIRDS, POLAR BEARS, UNICORN, PENGUIN, FACE PAINTING

When they rode the carousel
and Annie got a brown horse,
Grandpa traded with her because
he said his was too pink.

Finally, they stopped at the playground.

"I'm too hot," said Grandpa.
"You kids play here while I rest."
"Hooray!" Gregory said.
All the kids ran to the playground.

When they got home. Gregory's mom met them at the door.
"How was the zoo?" she asked.

"It was great!" said Gregory with a wide grin. "We saw baboons
and rode camels and had our faces painted. And Grandpa shared his
candy and his ice cream and his horse with my friends!"

Gregory's mom smiled at Grandpa. "You're such a good-hearted grump," she said fondly. "That's too much praise for me." Grandpa frowned. "Just thank the Lord it didn't rain!"

That night, Grandpa tucked Gregory into bed.

"Dear Lord," Grandpa prayed, "thank you for our day together at the zoo, even though it was too hot, too tiring, too messy, too bumpy, too pink, and too smelly for me."

Gregory giggled. "And thank you, Lord, for my Grandpa Grumpy," he said, squeezing his grandpa's hand. "He's kind of grumpy, but I love him so much. Amen."

"Well, now I've got too much love," exclaimed Grandpa. "You take some of it, Gregory." And he wrapped his arms around Gregory in a big bear hug.